D0251189

NEW MOUSE CITY
SEWER DEPT.

Dear Mouse Friends,
Welcome to the world of

Geronimo Stilton

NEW MOUSE CITY
1
2
3
4
5
6
7
8
9
10
11
12
13
14
15
16
17
18
19
20
21
22
23
24
25
26
ANOTHER FINE MAP FROM CLOSE ENOUGH MAP CO.

1. Cheese Factories
2. Angorat International Airport
3. Comic Book Store
4. Mouse General Hospital
5. WRAT Radio & Television Station
6. Snotnose Castle
7. Cheese Market
8. Manhole #13
9. Grand Hotel
10. Botanical Gardens
11. Petunia Pretty Paws's House
12. *The Daily Rat*
13. *The Rodent's Gazette*
14. Thea's House
15. Cheap Junk for Less
16. Geronimo's House
17. Benjamin's House
18. Public Library
19. Mousidon Square Garden
20. Hercule Poirat's Office
21. New Mouse Harbor
22. Beach
23. Curlyfur Island Amousement Park
24. Shipyard
25. Luna Light House
26. The Statue of Liberty

Geronimo Stilton
THE GRAPHIC NOVEL
THE SEWER RAT STINK

with
Tom Angleberger
story by
Elisabetta Dami
color by Corey Barba

An Imprint of
SCHOLASTIC

Published by Scholastic Inc., *Publishers since 1920,* 557 Broadway, New York, NY 10012. SCHOLASTIC and associated logos are trademarks and/or registered trademarks of Scholastic Inc.

Stilton is the name of a famous English cheese. It is a registered trademark of the Stilton Cheese Makers' Association. For more information, go to stiltoncheese.com.

"National Anthem of the Sewers" adapted and composed by Oscar Angleberger

ISBN 978-1-338-58730-2

Text by Geronimo Stilton
Story by Elisabetta Dami
Original title *La strano caso della pantegana puzzona*
Cover and Illustrations by Tom Angleberger
Edited by Abigail McAden and Tiffany Colón
Translated by Emily Clement
Color by Corey Barba
Lettering by Shivana Sookdeo and Kristin Kemper
Book design by Phil Falco and Shivana Sookdeo
Creative Director: Phil Falco
Publisher: David Saylor

10 9 8 7 6 5 4 3 2 1 20 21 22 23 24

Printed in China 38
First edition, May 2020

TABLE OF

CONTENTS

CHAPTER ONE

GORGONZOLA, STINKY SOCKS, OR . . . CAT PEE?

Oh...I forgot to introduce myself! My name is
Stilton...

Geronimo Stilton!

I'm the publisher of THE RODENT'S GAZETTE!
THE RODENT'S GAZETTE
It was a...
But I'm also writing a novel. Its title will be...

WHAT A STINK!

No that's not the title of my novel! That's what I said because:

Something smelled

AWFUL!

My whiskers curled up in disgust!!!

It smells like
ROTTEN
GORGONZOLA.*
*Gorgonzola is a kind of cheese.

Smells more like DIRTY SOCKS.

Nope! It's CAT pee!

Banana
Sour milk!
Alien skunks!
Month old turkey sandwich
Moldy meat!
Diaper monster!

The only thing everybody could agree on was...

There was one mouse who liked it...

$20?!!? For one clothespin? That deal stunk almost as bad as the mystery smell!
I headed back inside!

But the next day the smell was worse!

And the next day... even worse!!

CHAPTER TWO

STRANGE! VERY STRANGE!

I stayed inside for A WEEK, hoping the **STENCH** would go away, but...

THAT'S **RIDICULOUS**!
I was out 50 **BUCKS**!
But at least I could walk around New Mouse City again...

At first, I saw FOR SALE signs everywhere. But as I got closer to the center of town...

And where did they get enough MONEY?

HONK!

Suddenly...

EEK!

STRANGER AND STRANGER!

Another week passed...and it still STANK! Everyone I knew had left New Mouse City!

I gave both of these a paws-up!

Meanwhile, I let all the employees of **THE RODENT'S GAZETTE** go on vacation.

There was no one left in **NEW MOUSE CITY** to read the newspaper!

I was starting to think about leaving, too. Not only was I **LONELY**, but the **SMELL** had crept into my office.

IT_

I couldn't even type because I was busy holding my **NOSE!**

P.U.!

THAT'S IT!
A mouse can only take so much!
I'm going home to pack!
GERONIMO STILTON EDITOR
SLAM!

CHAPTER FOUR

OH...UH... I'M SURE IT'S NOTHING

I walked home, looking at my BEAUTIFUL town for what might be the last time!

But I'm not the bravest mouse...
And being all alone in an empty city was getting...
CREEPY!
rustle

I whirled around...
but no one was there...
just the trees!

GREAT GALLOPING GOUDA*!

*Gouda is a type of cheese.

Running from trees? I've got to get a grip!

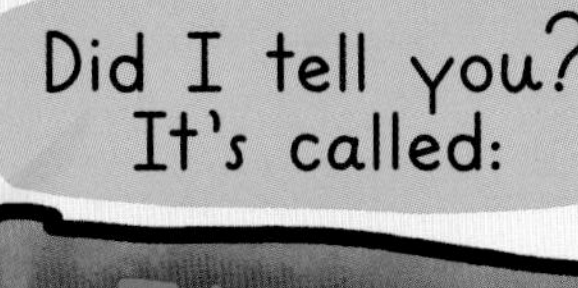

NO, THAT'S NOT THE NAME OF THE NOVEL! THAT'S WHAT WAS REALLY HAPPENING!

CHAPTER FIVE

TRAPPED ...BY A TREE?

I was so scared, I ran right past my house!

For one thing...banana trees don't grow in New Mouse City! And even if they did, they wouldn't say:

PSSST! GERONIMO!

How do you like my disguise?

I groaned!
It was my old pal:

HERCULE POIRAT!

I'd know that silly **MUSTACHE** anywhere!

Oh, I know who you are, Gerry Berry! In fact, I've been LOOKING for you!

Oh no!

THE MYSTERIOUS STINK!

He said it...

I started walking home. Hercule followed me, of course!

What? Who are you even talking about?

I'm talking about everybody who had to leave New Mouse City!

Your friends, your family, your newspaper staff, and...my one true love, your sister, Thea!

Just then, my phone buzzed...

BENJAMIN
The mountains are nice, but I want to come home to New Mouse City! I miss you, Uncle!

I'LL DO IT!!

I can help you <u>and</u> my friends, <u>and</u> save New Mouse City!

And it'll be such a

it will put the paper back in business and...

Hold on, Gerry Berry! We have to solve this mystery first. Let's go to my office and make a plan.

CHAPTER SIX

A VERY NEAT LITTLE PLACE!

Hercule's office is a GRUNGY LITTLE building between two SKYSCRAPERS.

How do you like my anti-spy tomato sauce, Gerry Berry?

It's red on red. Nobody will even notice.

Gee, you haven't changed a bit, Gerry Berry! You always were a fussy little mouse!

*Ricotta is a type of cheese.

It was a DUMP!

It was a DISASTER!

It was crawling with FLEAS!

CHAPTER SEVEN

NO, THANK YOU!

Bananas, garlic, pickle-ripple ice cream! So healthy!

GLUB GLUB GLUB

BURP!

Can we just get started solving the mystery?

Sure! Give me one second to find the map!

CHAPTER EIGHT

3 HOURS LATER!

After three hours, two more smoothies, and 347 flea bites...

MANHOLES OF THE
NEW MOUSE
CITY
SEWER
PETUNIA PRETTY PAWS'S HOUSE
RODENT
ANGORAT AIRPORT
MANHOLE #13
PARK
CHEESE MARKET
THEA'S HOUSE
THE RODENT'S GAZETTE
CHEAP JUNK FOR LESS
RIVER
DAILY RODENT
GERONIMO'S HOUSE
BENJAMIN'S HOUSE
PUBLIC LIBRARY
MOUSIDON SQUARE
GARDE
HARBOR
BEACH
LUNA LIGHT HOUSE
= MANHOLE
Instructions:
To open manhole, turn in direction that Grant Gentlemouse, founder of New Mouse City, is facing.
NEW MOUSE CITY
SEWER

But...manholes only lead into...
THE SEWER!

Exactly! Let's go!

You're not
REALLY
going into the sewer, are you???
Of course!

I've always wanted to see what's down there!

Well, I have
NOT!

I'm not taking another st-

Gerry Berry!! You found the first one! Great job!!

I didn't mean to!

And now we take a big whiff!

SNORT

For the next seven hours, Hercule and I checked every manhole until there was just one left: #13!

This is the clue we've been looking for!
Someone filled these balloons with foul air in the sewer, then brought them **out** here. So we will go **in** here!

We're not really actually going in that hole, are we???

Of course not!
Whew!
Not until we pack some bananas for the trip!

CHAPTER NINE

20 POUNDS of BANANAS!

Hercule was right about one thing...always pack wisely before starting an adventure!

This is my pack...

This is Hercule's

Twenty pounds of bananas?
15
10
20
For a snack!

A battery-powered mini fridge?
To keep the bananas fresh.

A jumbo bottle of stomach pills?
2,000
GAS-GAS GO-AWAY!
You'll understand after we eat twenty pounds of bananas.

A teddy bear?
He's my lil' fuzzy wuzzy buddy! Yes, he is!

A baby blanket?
I can't sleep without it.

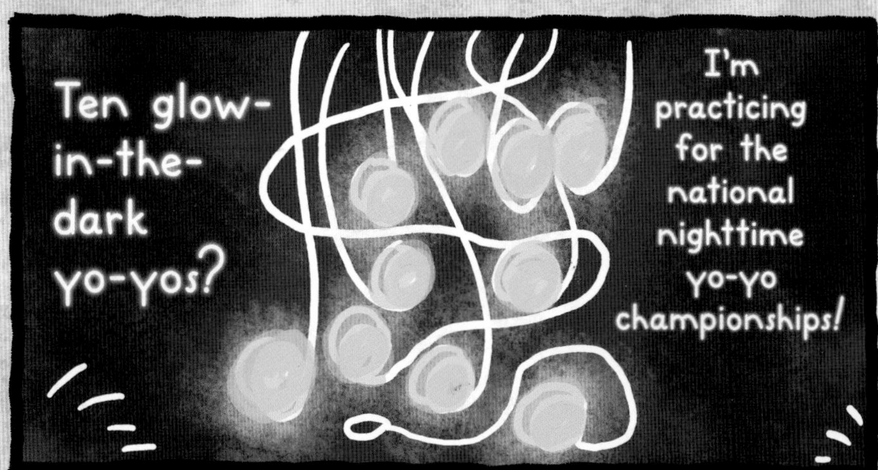
Ten glow-in-the-dark yo-yos?
I'm practicing for the national nighttime yo-yo championships!

Your collection of DOG MOUSE books?
I'm hoping you'll read me a bedtime story!
DOG MOUSE
DOGMOUSE ♥
DOG MOUSE IN LOVE
RETURN OF DOG MOUSE

A flower vase?
A dear memory of my favorite aunt!

A record player?! And records?!
It was hard choosing just ten albums to bring.

Knitting supplies?
Knitting calms my nerves.
YARN

A...What is that, anyway?
An antique chamber pot!

You mean a...
A fancy portable toilet, yes!

ENOUGH!
I give up! Take whatever you want! As long as I don't have to carry it!
Great! Just let me get my
PERUVIAN STAMP COLLECTION
and I'll be ready!

CHAPTER TEN

SECOND PLACE

Finally, Hercule finished packing and we headed back to manhole #13...

Whoever can open this manhole first wins a prize!

What's the prize?

Hercule doesn't know it, but I got tired of Trap calling me a wimp, so I started working out!

One pound

One ounce

I may not be a MUSCLE MOUSE, but I know I can lift a manhole cover!

STRAIN
STOMPY STOMP STOMP
PAIN

I GIVE UP!
Too bad, Gerry Berry! You should have used brains not muscles!
WHAT?!?

Instructions: Top open manhole, turn in direction that Grant Gentlemouse, founder of New Mouse City, is facing.
Yep! Next time read the directions!
Right here on the map!

See? All I have to do is spin it in the direction Grant is facing!

NEW MOUSE CITY SEWER DEPT.

SPIN

POP!

And it pops right off! I win the race! And you get second place.

Here, you hold the manhole cover while I help you put on your prize.

Standing there in the STENCH, holding all that HEAVY stuff, I thought things couldn't get worse!

EEK!

OW!
CRUNCH!

OOF!

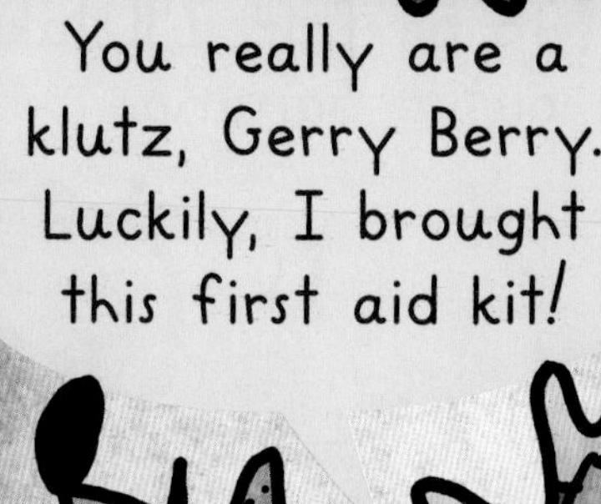
You really are a klutz, Gerry Berry. Luckily, I brought this first aid kit!

groan

CHAPTER ELEVEN

LUCKY NUMBER 13

Of course I didn't want to go...but then I remembered that it was the only way to help my friends. So...

MOLDY

MOZZA-

RELL-

AAAAAAAA

SPLMASH

Is my teddy bear okay?

Somehow, Hercule's backpack landed on a pile of nice, soft balloons...

I had **NOT!**

Look! More of those empty balloons!

SNIFF!

P.U.! Well, this proves it!

Someone used these balloons to poison the air of New Mouse City!

The answer to that question lies...

DEEPER IN THE SEWER!

CHAPTER TWELVE

Hercule flipped over his map. On the other side was a map of the sewer tunnels. Miles and miles of them!!!

We're right here...

So...let's see... That's: four rights, two lefts, then zigzag through the grease trap, around the bend, right at the fork, left into Drain #37, left, then right. Easy!

An hour later...

Do you know where we are?

Of course!

Two hours later...

Do you know where-

Definitely?

Three hours later...

Do-

Nope!

DOESN'T MATTER???

Nope... It's like Einstein said... Everything is relative.

Did you hear that?

Footsteps!!!

splish... splosh...

splish... splosh...

splish... splosh...

What kind of **CREATURE** would be splashing around this **DEEP IN THE SEWER?** I did <u>not</u> want to find out!

CHAPTER THIRTEEN

THE USUAL STUFF

Tripwires...

WHOA

TRIP!

...hidden switches....

OOOF

CLICK

...trapdoors.

AAAAH!!

Is my teddy bear okay?
KA THUN KA

And where's that light coming from?
KA THUN KA

And what's that weird noise?
KA THUN KA

GET DOWN HERE!

Is that...
MONEY?
THUN KA
THUN KA
THUN KA
SUE WHIRATZ INC. $

I don't get it, Gerry Berry! If you landed in a big pile of MONEY, why are you so upset?

First of all, it's fake money! Second of all...

LOOK BEHIND YOU!

Prepare to meet...

SHE WHO RULES THE UNDER-WORLD!

CHAPTER FOURTEEN

THE LADY OF THE SEWERS

The rat with the spear forced us to walk deeper into the sewers...until...

Are you ready to meet our queen?

You mean Sue Whiratz?

Sue Whiratz?
HA HA HA HA!
Silly mouse!
We're all
"Sue Whiratz"!
Get it?
Sewer rats?
And our queen is...

The Lady of the Sewers!
The Duchess of Rubbish!
The most foul vermin of the noble dynasty of STINK!
Her Royal Majesty...
TRASHFUR SPARKLES XIII

As we approached the throne, I realized it was made from trash! And so was the queen's outfit!

CHAPTER FIFTEEN

THE SONG OF THE SEWERS!

From all sides, more rats emerged from the shadows! Many of them had musical instruments...

WITH FEELING

We live in the sew-ers where

peo-ple throw their trash!

No one knows that we ex-ist in this

maze of dregs and ash!

We love our stink, we love our queen,

our teeth are nice shades of yel-**LOW!**

We love our dark world be- LO-O-O-O-W!

CHAPTER SIXTEEN

EVERYBODY LOVES TO DANCE!

After the national anthem all the rats were smiling. So I thought everything was okay. But...

Then who are you?

My name is Stilton...
Geronimo Stilton!
I run THE RODENT'S GAZETTE.

And my friend is HERCULE POIRAT, the famouse detective!
Aw shucks.

A detective and a newsmouse? You sound like...
SPIES!

GRAB THEM!

I was scared! I was terrified! I was frozen from fear of being grabbed by angry sewer rats!

and plugged them into the speaker part of the throne!

EVERYBODY LOVES TO DANCE!

BOOGIE WOOGIE SHOOGIE DOO DOO

M'lady, may I have this dance?

Yes... dance, beautiful queen!

Let the music move you! Forget your troubles; forget the spies!
DANCE and be HAPPY!

At last,
the last record
was over...

And I enjoyed dancing with you despite your smell!

old fish

GUARDS! PERFUME HIM!

rotten egg

dirty-sock juice

What did you say your name was again?

Hercule.

I think I'll call you...HERKY!

Yes...I think I like you, Herky! So I'm not going to put you in jail...

I'm going to...

Hercule turned pale! He squeaked! He groaned! He whimpered!

I can't marry her, Gerry Berry! She's beautiful, but...

SSSSSHH! If the queen hears you, we'll both be thrown in jail!

Luckily, she didn't hear because she was holding a meeting with a **SCARY** gang of sewer rats!

I call forth the GRAND COUNCIL!

GAGA REFLEXA
COCO P. FUNGUSNOOT
SMELBA TOOTENPOOT
CONTESSA FLUSHALOO
MADAM MOIST
CLOGGY JO
VAPORIA
RITA REEKA!
Bob

Members of the Grand Council! The royal plan is almost ready for the final phase!

Hip Hip Hoo-rat!

WRONG!!

Now, listen up, while I repeat it!

STEP 1:

Fill balloons with super strong sewer stink.

old cabbage
moldy garlic
burnt popcorn
wet rat hair
rotten eggs
decomposing diapers
sewer algae

STEP 2:

Release the stink into New Mouse City through Manhole #13.

STEP 3:

All the mice will sell their homes and move away from the smell.

STEP 4:

We buy up their empty homes using phony money we printed!

STEP 5!!!

Find a rat to make my king with whom I will rule! Take over New Mouse City! Take over Mouse Island! Take over...

THE WORLD!!!

LONG LIVE THE DYNASTY OF STINK!

Hercule hadn't heard her because he was using my phone.

WHO ARE YOU CALLING?
WHO'S THEA? A LADY MOUSE?!
NEVER AGAIN!
DO NOT MAKE ME JEALOUS!
I wonder if the warranty covers evil sewage queen stompings?
CRACK!

Curds and curses! I'd just lost my last link with my friends! Could things get any worse? (Yes.)

I call for a vote! Do you council members approve of Hercule to be my husband and your new KING?

Which one of us gets to marry the other one?

The...
...other...
gulp
...one?

No...I mean...I'm flattered of course...but...

When I marry it must be for LOVE!

But I do LOVE you!
Same here!
I ♥ him most!
I ♥ him more!
No, I do!
Me!
Ditto!
Gimme that mouse!

Whoever catches it gets Stilton!

WOO-HOO!

YAY!

"Wedding tonight"?

"Gets Stilton"?

CHAPTER NINETEEN
WELCOME TO SEWER CITY!

The queen ordered the council to get the throne room ready for a ROYAL WEDDING!

Since Sewer City has canals, not roads, we'll take my gondola. Stilton! You may row us!

Me?

Look around! We have it all here!
All thrown away by you wasteful mice above!

There's the floating recycler's market! They can make anything out of old cans and plastic bottles!

A water bottle becomes a flowerpot!
Plastic bags are woven into fabric!
ROYAL WEDDING 2 DAY
Old TVs and computers are upgraded!

And there's the power plant where sewer gas is turned into free electricity!

It's not all work! We love to play all kinds of sports...

Especially WATER sports!

Cesspool sailing

Sludge skiing

100M rat style

and Synchronized swimming!

We even have airplanes! Tossed out by you, but fixed by us! Did you know I have a pilot's license?

CHAPTER TWENTY

BATS! BUGS! SLUGS!

Hercule had found the way out, but we had no chance of trying an escape. We had just arrived at:

This'll be our little love nest, Herky!

It was dark inside, but there was just enough light for me to see...

BATS!

SLUGS!

BUGS!

Say hello to my pets: Snickers the bat, Sluggins the Third, and Bruno!

CHAPTER TWENTY-ONE

NEWS FROM NEW MOUSE CITY

The queen led us through room after room of broken furniture and recycled junk. It actually had a certain charm. Then a new rat ran in...

Your Highness! I have important news from above!

You boys enjoy the indoor pool, while I talk with the prime minister!

Gerry Berry! You gotta get me out of this wedding!

But first we gotta get out of this POOL!

IT REALLY STINKS!

The real estate deals are done! We now own ALL of New Mouse City, except for two properties.
Excellent work, Barbara! Now tell me...Who owns the last two?

Let's see... A G. Stilton and an H. Poirat.
G.STILTON
H.POIRAT

No problem! Those two will be ours after tonight's weddings!

Soon we will have it all!
hee hee
ha ha

SNORT
YUK YUK YUK
HA HA HA HA!
giggle

MWAH
HA HA

CHAPTER TWENTY-TWO

ROYAL BEAUTY SECRETS

The queen clapped her hands, and a swarm of rats grabbed us. I thought they were going to clobber us, but they just wanted to get us ready for the wedding!

Another rat put mud packs on our faces. The mud was crawling with

WORMS!

Then they sprayed us with the queen's special perfume: EXPIRED!

It was very, very, very old milk!

Then the queen went to change into her wedding dress.
Don't move, boys... I'll be right back.

Could this be our chance to escape?

And when I say don't move, I mean
DON'T MOVE!

Watch 'em, Bruno!
We didn't move!

CHAPTER TWENTY-THREE

HERE COMES THE BRIDE

We didn't move. For one hour we just sat there waiting while Bruno growled at us. Then a band began to play.

Here comes the
BRIDE,
all dressed in two-ply, with old sushi on the forks in her crown!

Psst...Gerry Berry! You've got to help me...I can't marry her...You know my true love is Thea!
It doesn't look like you have a choice!
My heart is breaking... and that's not something that can be fixed.
I'm sorry, old friend. It–
AAAH!
GET MOVIN', MICE!

CHAPTER TWENTY-FOUR

THE OLD FLYING-BANANA TRICK!

The queen ordered us to climb into the royal carriage.

Hercule and I climbed into the carriage, while the queen spoke to a cheering crowd.

Oh no! There's no way out of this!

Well... there is one way.

No! No! Not that! Not the old flying-banana trick!
Anything but the old flying-banana trick!

Yes...the old flying-banana trick. If it doesn't work, tell Thea that I loved her to the end.

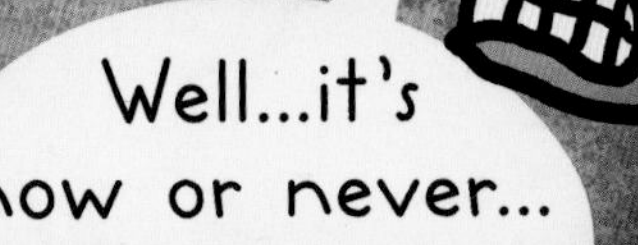
Well...it's now or never...

LOOK!
A FLYING BANANA!

Where?
Oh my stars!
Huh?
Outta my way!
Wow!
Lemme see!
Is that it?
I don't see it.

While the rats were distracted, Hercule jumped into the driver's seat and grabbed the reins...

Hold on, Gerry Berry!

GIDDYUP! H'YAH!!

CHAPTER TWENTY-FIVE

A BUMPY RIDE

Hercule drove the carriage right down the big garbage pile that the palace sat on!

This player piano is connected to the wheels!

So the faster we go, the faster it plays!

It's playing Mousezart's Fourth Sonata! Isn't it lovely?

OH NO!

Don't get me wrong... I like Mousezart's music as much as anymouse in New Mouse City.

HOOKED ON MOUSEZART

But the music was TOO FAST!

The ride was TOO BUMPY!

And the edge of the cliff was TOO CLOSE!

*Ricotta is a type of cheese.

LIGHT THUMP

Gerry Berry! Stop fooling around! We gotta get out of here!

The queen hasn't given up!
GASP!

GET THEM!

Paddle, Gerry Berry, paddle!

MANHOLE #13

Gerry! You're paddling the wrong way!
MANHOLE #13

I'm paddling the right way! It's the current!
Uh-oh...

It's just too strong!
DANGER

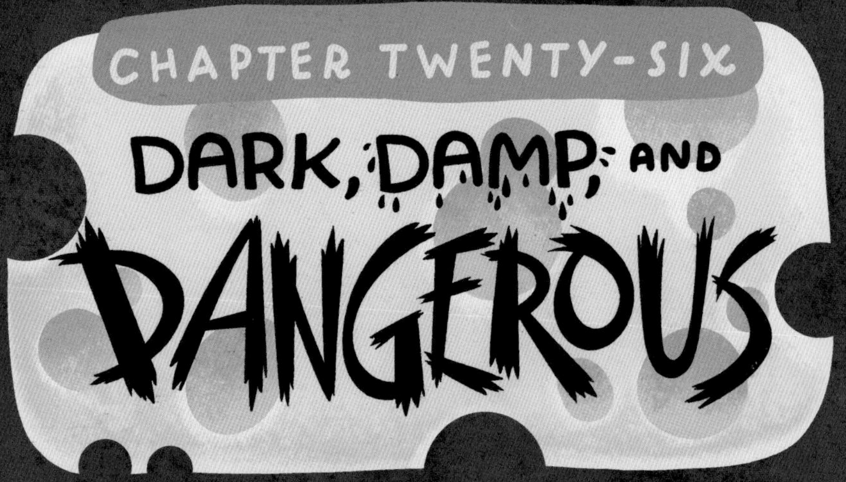

The current dragged us into the pipes! It was like a maze! At least, I think it was! It was so dark I couldn't really tell!

Oh no! It's pitch-dark and we left the flashlight with the backpacks in the throne room!

And I left my teddy bear!!

SOB

Hey! A light!
We're saved!

No...we're
caught!

What do
we do?
We either go
back and marry
sewer rats...

Or we try to dive
underwater until they pass!

Look! There's the boat.

EMPTY!

LIGHTSHIP

The rats were wrong! We weren't being dragged downstream...We were being dragged
DOWN THE DRAIN!

The drain dragged us down and around and upside down until it spat us and the sewer water out into a...

GIANT WATER-FALL!

Isn't this fun, Gerry Berry?

No, I don't think this is any fun at all!

We landed right in the middle of the sewer rats' watersports lagoon!

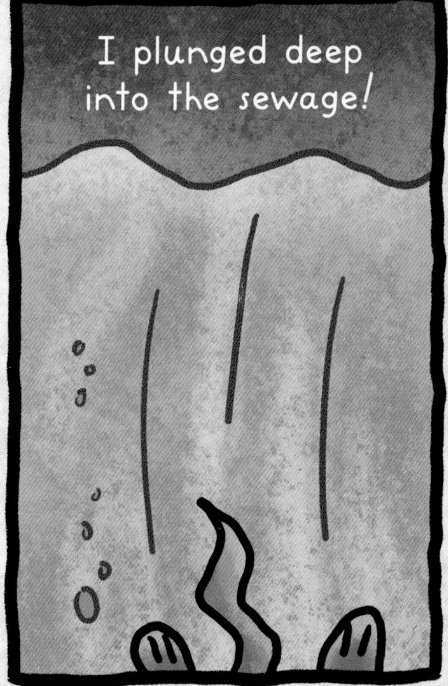

I
sank...

Then suddenly:
a lifeline!

It was
Hercule!

I was wrong to yell at him earlier... Here he was pulling me to safety with...

A JET SKI?

Hang on, GB!

splutter

VROOM

SMACKO

What? My feet are <u>not</u> big! Only slightly larger than the average mouse, but certainly not big! I'm sorry to be rude, but the fact is that <u>your</u> feet are bigger th
And even if my
I'll ask you not t
yelling about the

JUST DO IT!

CHAPTER TWENTY-EIGHT

LOOK BEHIND YOU!

Once I got my normal-sized feet under me, I was able to water-ski...well, actually,

-ski!

No! In fact, I have to speed up!

What? Why?

Look behind you!

Hercule stomped on the gas pedal, and we zoomed across the lagoon! I was so HAPPY when I saw the exit up ahead!

But I was so UNHAPPY when I saw Hercule take the wrong tunnel!

CHAPTER TWENTY-NINE

WELCOME TO SEWER CITY! Again!

We zoomed out of the tunnel and right into downtown Sewer City...with an angry queen and her guards in hot pursuit!

And then, Hercule took a turn too tight!

Hercule

Me

sidewalk

little old lady

My feet were so coated in sewer GOO that I SLID right across the sidewalk and into...

SLAM

Why you rotten, no-good, cheese-brained, knock-kneed whipper-snapper!

I'm <u>so</u> sorry! Normally I try to be a very polite mouse!

But then I saw something even scarier blocking the sidewalk up ahead:

BRUNO!

CHAPTER THIRTY

JUST LIKE THE CURLYFUR ISLAND AMOUSEMENT PARK WATERSKI STUNT SPECTACULAR!

Bruno was blocking the whole sidewalk! And I couldn't stop! There was only one thing to do...

*Conveniently located pizza boxes.

It was just like the Curlyfur Island Water-Ski Stunt Spectacular! (A show I've seen fifty-seven times!)

I SOARED over...

Bruno

two guards

A cheese smoothie stand

CUP O' CURDZ

Bob

Meanwhile, outside the throne room...

CHAPTER THIRTY-ONE

IT'S JUST LIKE Nibblin' Cheese!

Did I faint? Was I knocked out? All I can remember is waking up, covered in fish-flavored icing, with Hercule yelling at me!

There they are!
STOP them!

Now put on my pack and
GO!

Please don't say you're going to fly us out of here!
Please don't say you're going to fly us out of here!
Please don't say you're going to fly us out of here!
Please don't say you're going to

You think you can fly one of <u>those</u>???

They look like bats!

Of course! It's just like nibblin' cheese!

Have I mentioned that:

A) I hate flying,

B) I hate flying with Hercule, and

C) I hate flying with Hercule in planes shaped like winged sewer mammals!!!

CHAPTER THIRTY-TWO

YOU CAN'T FLY A PLANE THROUGH A MANHOLE!

First we bumped into the roof! Then we dove down and skimmed over the sludge lagoon!

We're doomed!
We're... being followed!
We're lost!!

Yikes! Well, don't worry... we're almost to Manhole #13!

Manhole #13?!? Hercule! You can't fly a plane through a manhole!

We were shot up and out of the sewer through Manhole #13!

Wait...I forgot which way to turn it!

Uh...whichever way... the...uh...face is facing...no, wait, that was to unscrew it! So...try the way it's not facing...

CHAPTER THIRTY-THREE

ATTACK, MY VALIANT WARRIORS!

The queen climbed out, followed by a gang of her toughest fighters! (And Bob.)

The city is mine! Soon all of Mouse Island will be mine! But right now....

You two are mine!

Attack, my valiant warriors!

ATTACK!

Have I told you how beautiful sunrise is in New Mouse City?

The sun's pale rays gently kissed the city I call home.

Nooo! We will never conquer this bright world above!

Let us return to our dark world below!

You have not seen the last of Queen Trashfur Sparkles the Thirteenth!

...oh, and half a roll of toilet paper.

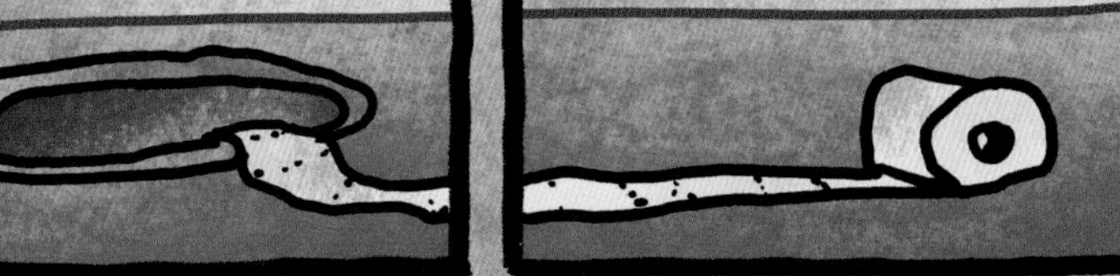

And then there was nothing* but silence.

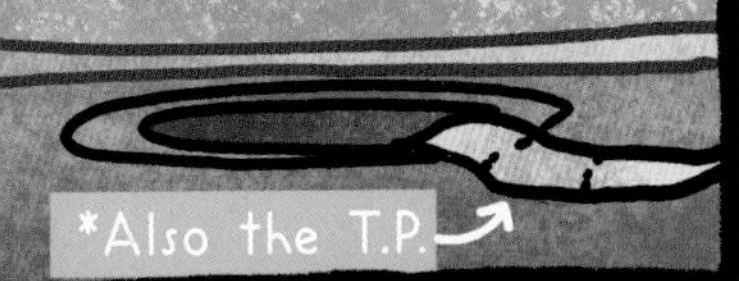

CHAPTER THIRTY-FOUR

37 BATHS AND 58 SHOWERS

The queen was gone and so was the stink! (Well, almost.)

We've got a story to write for **THE RODENT'S GAZETTE!**

After he had a couple of garlic-banana smoothies, Hercule perked up. We worked like wild mice to write a special edition!

THE RODENT'S GAZETTE

-SPECIAL EDITION-FREE-

SAFE TO COME BACK!

CITY SMELLS PRETTY GOOD!

By G. Stilton and H. Poirat

REAL ESTATE DEALS CANCELED!

Sue Whiratz Inc. used fake money!!!

See pg. 2

Of course, most mice were still out of town, so we published the story on our website, on SHOUTBOOK and SQUEAKR and everywhere else we could think of!

InstaPaw
Smells great-ish.

SNAPCHEESE
COME BAK!

And then Hercule took his nap, and I took thirty-seven baths and fifty-eight showers...

AHHH...

#23

CHAPTER THIRTY-FIVE

HIP, HIP, HOORAY!

All the mice who had fled New Mouse City saw the story and came back!

*Almost everyone

But the best was my nephew Benjamin!

I've got a great idea! Let's all go to **THE RODENT'S GAZETTE** and you can help me make a special report about the importance of recycling!

Woo-hoo!

This is literally a dream come true!

Even rad-i-cooler!

Do we get vests?

Can I come, too?

Water bottles take 100 to 1,000 years to decompose.

We're taking photos of ways to reuse scrap paper!

It's origami.

Mayor, what is New Mouse City doing to stop roadside litter?

It was a very special day...Seeing these young rodents so full of energy and curiosity gives me great hope for the future!

Soon the smell faded away completely, and life in New Mouse City returned to normal...

Finally! I can get back to writing my novel!

BUCKETS OF BANANA BARF!

BY G. STILTON

No, that's not the name of my novel!!! That's what Hercule was yelling as he ran into my office!

Gerry Berry! Guess who wrote me! Go ahead, guess! No! I'll tell you! It's from...

HER!

It was a dark and tasty cheese

VISIT BEAUTIFUL
SEWER
CITY!
HERKY...
I HAVE NOT FORGOTTEN YOU.
I WILL NEVER FORGET YOU.
IF YOU CHANGE YOUR MIND... YOU KNOW WHERE TO FIND ME!
XOXO TRASHFUR
HERKY POIRAT
NEW MOUSE CITY,
THE WORLD ABOVE
Ah... love!
THE END!

THE small PRINT!

?

WARRANTY
DEPT.

ABSOLUTE* UNLIMITED*
LIFETIME* WARRANTY*

*The Purchaser's phone shall be replaced by the
Seller at no charge with the following conditions:
Warranty is void if phone is damaged by cats dressed as
pirates, wrestlers, chefs, astronauts, or cats.
Warranty is void if phone is damaged by a smart-alecky cousin
engaged in pranks, shenanigans, antics, tricks, and/or high jinks.
Warranty is void if phone is damaged while chasing a yeti; exploring a
creepy castle; running from bulls; writing newspaper stories; or looking
for rubies, emeralds, diamonds, opals, or gems of any kind.
Warranty is void if phone is stomped on by an evil sewer queen with plans to
take over the world by releasing stink balloons into the city and marrying your best
friend, who can be annoying sometimes with all his bananas and mess and fleas and smelly
milkshakes, but he's really a great guy and he's in love with your sister, so he doesn't really want to marry
the sewer queen anyway. And he's using your phone to call your sister, but then the sewer queen hears him
and she's like STOMP and totally destroys your phone right there in the sewer. This warranty shall be void
if the phone is ever removed from its packaging or used for making phone calls, sending text messages, flipping
through MouseBook, ordering cheese or cheese-related products, or playing dumb, time-wasting games. Don't you have
anything better to do than play those dumb games? Gee whiz, read a book or something! And have you washed behind
your ears lately? And look what a mess your room is! Can't you even put your socks in the hamper? How long would
take? Five seconds? Okay, so you have hours to play those dumb games and chat with your friends but not five seconds
throw your socks in the hamper so the whole house doesn't stink? Warranty is void if we say it is. Oh, you think that's
unfair? Well, maybe you should have thought of that before you bought the phone, you big cheesehead! If you want a
new phone, you're going to pay for it! And guess what? You're going to pay too much for it! Ha ha! That's how we
You don't like it? Too late! It's all here in the small print that you skimmed over two years ago when you bought
phone!!! Maybe you shouldn't have been in such a big rush, huh, Cheddarface? Oh, you mice are all alike. You
give you free phones and not eat you. Well, forget it! We're cats! That's what we do! Well, that and lick
how we take baths. Do you have a problem with that, mouse? I didn't think so. So, where was
about this weird dream I had last night. See, I was waiting in line to buy something,
wanted it really badly because I was waiting in the line for hours! And then all
sewer. And there was this whole city down there with buildings and
and you were there. Maybe it wasn't a dream, but I sure am
was standing in line for! Coconuts. But it turned
hey, I don't even like coconuts! Oh
about the texture. I hate the
really like to eat? M

his warranty shall be void if the phone is ever removed from its packaging or used for making phone calls,
ending text messages, flipping through MouseBook, ordering cheese or cheese-related products or playing
dumb, time-wasting games. Don't you have any to do than play those dumb games? Gee whiz,
ead a book or something! And have lately? And look what a mess your
oom is! Can't you even put that take? Five seconds? Okay,
ou have hours to play t not five seconds to throw
our socks in the ha

Warranty is void should have thought of
hat before you b ead! If you want a new
hone, you're g ? You're going to pay
oo much for it 't like it? Too late! It's
ll here in the d over two years ago
when you boug you shouldn't have be
n such a big ru give you free phones a
ot eat you. W That's what we do! Wel
hat and lick ou with that, mouse? I
idn't think so. am I had last night. See, I w
aiting in line to anted it really badly because I
as waiting in the li ough a manhole into the sewer.
And there was this whol d stuff, and you were there, and you
ere there, and you were the ure am glad I'm home, because there's no
lace like home, Coco. That's what I was conuts. But it turned out they were out of
oconuts and I was mad, but then I woke up and I was don't even like coconuts! Oh, you don't
ike coconuts either? Right, it's not the flavor. I love the something about the texture. I hate thos

void if phone is stomped by an evil sewer queen

KiDS!

TEACH 'EM TRICKS!

Have you ever wanted a loving pet like BRUNO™?

CALL 'EM BY NAME!

IMPRESS YOUR FRIENDS!

ACTUAL SIZE

Here's your chance!

Visit Sewer City Pets today and buy our

COCKROACH STARTER KIT

for just $14.99!

Includes:

* One packet of cockroach eggs–guaranteed to hatch!
* Moldy bread!
* Stale bread!
* Bread!
* Tiny nametags...What will you name your new friends?

¢HEAP JUNK FOR LE$$

=YOUR PRANK SUPERSTORE=

OUR PROMISE: We test every prank on our cousin before we will sell it! Guaranteed yuks!

HIGHLIGHTS OF HERCULE'S RECORD COLLECTION

CATS
ACTUALLY JUST MICE IN MASKS!

SMASHMOUSE
CHEESEBALL-STAR

RHODY RODENT
SONGS TO KISS TO!

RAT + ROLL!
SNAP MY TRAP!

BOB SINGS:
SONGS OF BOB

ANGELA
& HER MUSICAL NOSE
2 HOURS of NOSE JAZZ!

DON'T MISS ANY ORIGINAL

OF GERONIMO'S ADVENTURES!

Geronimo Stilton

is an author and the editor-in-chief of *The Rodent's Gazette*, New Mouse City's most popular newspaper. He was awarded the Ratitzer Prize for his investigative journalism and the Anderson 2000 Prize for Personality of the Year. His books have been published all over the world. He loves to spend all his spare time with his family and friends.